KAH-LAN
and the
STINK-INK

KAREN AUTIO

illustrated by Emma Pedersen

CP | CRWTH PRESS

Library and Archives Canada Cataloguing in Publication

Title: Kah-Lan and the stink-ink / Karen Autio; illustrated by Emma Pedersen.

Names: Autio, Karen, author. | Pedersen, Emma, 1988- illustrator.

Identifiers: Canadiana (print) 20200264621 |
Canadiana (ebook) 20200264710 | ISBN 9781989724071

(softcover) | ISBN 9781989724088 (EPUB)

Classification: LCC PS8601.U85 K34 2020 | DDC jC813/.6—dc23

Copy-edited by Dawn Loewen
Proofread by Audrey McClellan
Cover and interior design by Teresa Bubela

Crwth Press
#204 – 2320 Woodland Drive
Vancouver, BC V5N 3P2
www.crwth.ca

MIX
Paper from
responsible sources
FSC® C103214
FSC
www.fsc.org

To Lindsaye Akhurst, Rescue Centre Manager,
Dr. Martin Haulena, Staff Veterinarian,
and the rest of the staff and volunteers
at Vancouver Aquarium's Marine
Mammal Rescue Centre—thank you
for your important work

S. D. G.

⁓

Let the sea resound, and everything in it,
the world, and all who live in it.

—Psalm 98:7 (New International Version)

Chapter One

Kah-Lan speed-weaves between green sea-tree bulbs. He pumps his webbed hind flippers, pushing against the water.

Kah-Lan is as large as his mother. He is the oldest male in his raft, and he's stronger than ever. He yearns to leave the raft of female sea otters and pups. Kah-Lan can't wait to explore the coastal waters.

But not alone.

1

Can he convince the next oldest male to leave with him? He finds Myac and charges into him, bunting him toward open sea. Myac leaps over sea-tree blades and dashes off underwater. Kah-Lan chases his bubble trail, paddling hard with his flippers.

A wave of excitement washes over Kah-Lan as he remembers spring, when he and Yamka, a female otter his age, left the hungry raft. They found big crabs to eat. But then the current at the point dragged them far out to sea. An orca hunted them—they could have been sea-meat—but they escaped.

Now, many dawns after their journey, Yamka ignores Kah-Lan. She will likely never leave the raft again. His mother ignores him too, and he can no longer resist the urge to leave.

Before Kah-Lan catches up to the faster male, Myac somersaults and dives under him. Myac swims back toward the raft, like they're playing a game of race-and-chase.

Kah-Lan streaks through the water to get alongside Myac. He bunts Myac again to turn him around. Kah-Lan also butts Wanu out of their sea-tree forest. Wanu squeals and tries paddling back to the sea-trees. Kah-Lan again butts him into open water and nips his tail.

Both younger otters turn on Kah-Lan, play-biting his face and neck. All they want to do is wrestle. Frustrated, Kah-Lan twists out of their reach. He rushes at each in turn, bumping them farther from shore.

Flipping around, Wanu speed-dives back toward the sea-tree forest. Kah-Lan pursues him underwater. Up ahead are the tall stems of sea-trees with their strong holdfast gripping the ocean floor.

Wanu is swimming straight at a giant octopus. It's not an enemy, but the water gets messy when an octopus is disturbed. If Wanu and Kah-Lan were at the surface, Kah-Lan could squeal a warning. But not underwater. Will Wanu see the creature in time?

Wanu darts at top speed without changing course.

At the last moment he veers away from the octopus. Scared, it squirts a cloud of black ink at Wanu. Then the octopus shoots a stream of water out of the mantle of its head, jetting away in the opposite direction.

Kah-Lan can't see Wanu through the inky water until Wanu churns it, clearing the ink. Kah-Lan follows him to the surface.

Wanu paddles toward the sea-trees, calling to his mother. Such a pup. Wanu is not ready to leave the raft.

When Kah-Lan approaches Myac again, Myac growls. Then Myac follows Wanu.

The younger males would rather race-and-chase and link paws with their mothers than set off with Kah-Lan. He gives up trying to convince them to go.

Kah-Lan launches out on his own. His belly is full of crab. His coat is well groomed and fluffed with air to keep his skin warm and dry.

More excited than anxious, Kah-Lan heads off along the coast. He travels in the direction of the hunting waters of a raft of male Elder otters. He'll be safer with a raft.

Kah-Lan takes a final look at the familiar land-trees on shore. Their dark green branches lean away from fierce ocean winds. He swims into the sunlight. While it's no longer summer-hot, it makes him blink. Closing his ears and nostrils, he slips beneath the surface.

Kah-Lan thrusts his flippers and ripples his body. He swiftly glides through the salt water.

The instinct to leave is so strong he forgets to give a last coo to Yamka and his mother. But he's not going back for anything.

Kah-Lan pumps the water harder, giddy with adventure. He speeds through the female raft's hunting waters. He pops up for a breath of air. Then onward he glides below the surface.

After travelling for a while, he remembers to look out for trouble. Having no Elder otters to warn him, he must be careful. Kah-Lan swims at the surface. Cresting a wave, he scans for dangers.

What will Kah-Lan find out here? Whirlpools? Orcas? He shudders. Those strange furless ones that walk on their hind legs? Despite prickles of concern, he feels a surge of energy and courage. No matter what's ahead, he can face it.

Kah-Lan gulps air and darts ahead. He rounds a point heaped with drift-trees. Then he steers between a small island and the shore. Kah-Lan swims and swims until his stomach rumbles. Soon he'll need to hunt for sea-meat.

Slam. A big wave dashes Kah-Lan backward against a sharp rock hidden below the surface. His heart thumps wildly. He has thick fur so his back only aches a little, but he could have scraped his nose on the rocks. How can Kah-Lan look out for every danger by himself? He misses the protection of his raft. Now he gazes out to sea, watchful for orcas.

The rocks are part of a reef. It's not a promising spot for food. Still Kah-Lan dives underwater to avoid the waves smashing him against rocks.

Are those purple mussels clinging to the reef down there? Kah-Lan paddles up to the surface to fill his lungs, then dives to find out. The closer he gets, the blacker they look.

Kah-Lan is disappointed to find only dark, jagged bits of rock. But what is that grey spotted object at the bottom? Are the spots a new kind of sea-meat? Kah-Lan deep-dives toward them.

The spotted object is smooth. Is it a rock? Kah-Lan approaches, reaches out his right paw and startles. The object has flippers at one end. It's a seal! But it's not moving. What's wrong with this seal?

Chapter Two

Kah-Lan paddles closer to the seal. The seal swishes its flippers, then slowly rises, eyes shut. Kah-Lan follows it upward, relieved it can swim.

When they are both at the surface, Kah-Lan is confused. The seal is breathing, but is it hurt? Kah-Lan grunts. The seal's eyes pop open and it snorts, moving away from him. It stares wide-eyed at Kah-Lan. Giving a calmer snort, it sinks and tucks itself under the reef. Kah-Lan gives the name Snort to the seal. Is Snort sleeping underwater? How long can Snort stay below?

Kah-Lan paddles around the reef. Soon he'll reach the males' hunting waters. There he can enjoy tasty crabs. But he's starting to feel weak and won't be able to swim that far without eating. To stay alive, he needs to eat a lot of sea-meat.

Diving, Kah-Lan finds sand and a few rocks. Clams might live here. Even with bulging his eyes to see better under-water, it's too dark to see well. His whiskers sense movement in the sand. Kah-Lan digs. His paws come up empty. After surfacing and filling his lungs, he makes another dive-and-dig.

Kah-Lan snatches several clams. He tucks some in the loose fold of skin under his left foreleg and the rest in his right pouch. Patting around in the sand until he finds a rock, Kah-Lan clutches it to his chest. The rock is flat and half as wide as him. He kicks toward the light.

At the surface, Kah-Lan flips onto his back. Grabbing a clam, he rapidly bashes it onto the rock. *Whack. Whack. Crack.*

He prefers crabs. But clams will do. Kah-Lan scrapes every bit of flesh out of the shell with his pointy teeth. Then he tosses it away and starts pounding another one. He turns his head so water doesn't splash in his eyes. It takes a lot of clams to fill his belly. After gobbling all of the clams, Kah-Lan does a roll-and-rinse, then dives to hunt again.

When he's no longer hungry, Kah-Lan grunts with contentment. *Ow-u-ugh.* He scrubs his chest. With his claws extended, he combs the bits of clam out of his fur. A few somersaults rinse his coat clean. He whisks the water to make bubbles and rubs them into his fur.

What an adventure—but Kah-Lan is tired from paddling and hunting. There are no sea-tree blades to wrap himself in to anchor him while he rests. Instead, Kah-Lan heads to a tiny island down the coast. He finds calm water in a nook between the boulders. It feels safe enough for him to sleep for a while. He covers his eyes with his paws.

~ↄ

The sun is directly overhead when Kah-Lan awakes. He yawns and stretches. All alone, he's anxious to reach the safety of the males' raft.

As he swims around a rocky point, an eagle soars above him. Kah-Lan is much too big to fear being carried off by the bird. But still he curves into the choppy waves. Gliding below the surface he can travel quickly.

With his next breath at the surface, he catches the scent of sea-trees. Not much farther to go. A burst of energy sends him whooshing under the waves.

The male Elder otters are resting in their sea-tree forest up ahead. They are all bigger than Kah-Lan. Will they let him join them?

Ow-u-ugh. Kah-Lan grunts for joy. The eyes of the closest males fly open. Kah-Lan hopes they'll grunt in return, signalling he can stay.

Instead, a silver-furred Grand otter growls. He charges at Kah-Lan, snarling.

The Grand otter's teeth are cracked and worn, but still Kah-Lan twists out of reach. He kicks his flippers to get away.

Now all of the males stare at Kah-Lan. Avoiding other Grand otters, Kah-Lan scouts for Elder otters with light brown head fur. Will younger Elders let him stay? He finds some partway along the raft and greets them.

They snarl at him too.

Kah-Lan's heart thuds. He doesn't want to be on his own.

He paddles around to the far edge of the raft. Kah-Lan grunts to the Elder otters resting there. One rushes at him, growling.

As Kah-Lan speeds away from the Elder otter, a wave of panic washes over him. He must leave. He won't have the protection of Elder males. He'll have to fend for himself. Every dawn and every dark. How can he survive all alone?

Kah-Lan takes off, his back end swishing up and down. When he reaches the hunting waters, he plunges deep, down to the ocean floor.

In the dim light he pats around with his paws. With his whiskers, he tries to sense crabs moving. There are none. Kah-Lan swims to a different spot and searches again. He feels a shell with his right paw. Kah-Lan grasps the crab before it can scuttle away.

Holding it against his chest with its pincers facing out, Kah-Lan kicks hard toward the sunlight. He bobs at the surface and leans back. He snaps off the crab's pincers and legs one at a time and slurps out the meat.

With no warning, a seagull swoops
in and grabs the last of the crab's legs
in its beak. Kah-Lan screams. The bird
steals the whole rest of the crab and
flaps away.

If Kah-Lan is warned about danger
by another otter's squeal, he can dive
holding on to his sea-meat. He knows one
otter can't see everything. He needs to
be part of a raft.

Nervous, he quickly gives his coat a light grooming and then paddles off.

Are there other young male sea otters around? They could help scout for dangers.

The sun is still fairly high in the sky. Kah-Lan travels farther along the coast. Light glints off something shiny ahead. There's a flash of black and white. Kah-Lan's heart pounds. Orca!

Chapter Three

Kah-Lan tenses. Where can he flee? The male otters' sea-tree forest is too far away.

Something moves on the orca's back. A furless one? How can it ride on an orca?

Kah-Lan looks closer. That's not a whale. It's one of the big shiny creatures that pass by the raft sometimes. They never attack. Still, he's wary of this one.

Kah-Lan swims around the shiny crea-ture at a safe distance. It doesn't bellow and lurch like some of them. It's quiet and still in the water. It holds its body stiff like all the rest. A whiff of a nasty smell makes Kah-Lan's nostrils twitch.

Another furless one appears, along with a furless pup. Both furless Elders lean over the water at the end of the shiny creature. There's a small hump partway out of the ocean—a grey spotted hump.

The furless ones are attacking Snort!

Kah-Lan squeals, warning Snort to escape, but the seal doesn't move. How can Snort sleep with furless ones so close? Is Snort alive?

Yes—Kah-Lan hears a soft snort. Kah-Lan screams a warning.

Urgent sounds burst out of a furless Elder's mouth: *Grab a knife.*

Kah-Lan can't make sense of its call, but the tone makes him frantic. He twists and turns, ever closer to Snort.

One of Snort's flippers is pressed flat against its body. The flipper is wrapped tightly with strands of fish-web. Kah-Lan grumbles. If the furless ones move away, he can snap the strands with his teeth.

They ignore him. Sunlight flashes off a pointy silver object in the paw of one of them. The furless Elder slips the point under a strand and jerks it upward, snapping the strand. The other furless Elder hauls fish-web away from Snort and onto the shiny creature.

More strands break. The furless Elder keeps gathering fish-web in its paws and cries: *I've got most of the net now.*

This call sounds less urgent. Kah-Lan paddles closer.

Snap.

With a final yank, the furless Elder falls backward, its paws full of fish-web.

Snort is free.

Snort glides toward Kah-Lan and nudges him. One furless Elder holds up a slim black object the size of its paw. *Click.*

Kah-Lan flinches, but the click doesn't hurt him.

Click.

Snort dives, speeding back in the direction of the reef where Kah-Lan found it sleeping. If Kah-Lan could raft with Snort they could help each other. But they need different sea-meat.

Left on his own, Kah-Lan whimpers in fright. What is lurking in the ocean? He breathes deeply and leaps into the waves, then paddles hard underwater.

Kah-Lan travels a long way. The beach he's passing is full of light grey drift-trees. His belly rumbles.

Gasp. A bad odour hits his nostrils. It's like the smell from the shiny creature, but worse. A floating drift-tree is extra shiny along its bottom edge. A rainbow-coloured trail follows the drift tree.

It's hard to see through, like octopus ink, and it stinks. Kah-Lan no longer feels hungry. He squeezes his nostrils shut. The stink-ink covers the water in the distance.

BOOM.

Kah-Lan jumps.

BOOM.

Chapter Four

Kah-Lan scans the area. A smooth yellow drift-tree and a red one like it rush toward him. Each is longer than two Grand otters swimming head to tail. A furless Elder sits inside each shiny drift-tree holding a straight branch with flipper-shaped ends.

One Elder screams: *Stay away, the fuel will hurt you.*

They slap the sides of their drift-trees with their paws. *BOOM. BOOM.*

Kah-Lan panics and flees.

Near shore on the other side of the bay, a young seagull flaps partly underwater. It gives a weak squawk. A rainbow sheen of stink-ink coats its grey feathers. The bird tries to fly but struggles.

A furless Elder arrives on the beach. It carries a web on a long branch and coos: *Let me help you, little bird. I'll clean your feathers.* It holds out the web toward the seagull.

Kah-Lan swims as close as he dares.

Sliding the web under the bird, the furless Elder lifts it out of the water and onto shore. It seems to be treating the seagull gently, but the web still frightens Kah-Lan.

His nose twitches from the bad smell. Kicking his flippers, he speeds away from the stink-ink.

When the air is fresh again, hunger gnaws Kah-Lan's insides. He slows, hunting for sea urchins clinging to rocks near shore. All he finds are green anemones wiggling their sticky tentacles. No sea-meat.

Leaving the rocks behind, Kah-Lan passes another beach. He sucks in air and speeds underwater.

A shadow covers Kah-Lan. He startles. Above him is a long dark shape. It's not black and white like an orca. Is it a new enemy about to attack?

Kah-Lan darts to the left. The dark shape turns in the same direction.

It's hunting Kah-Lan! He's going to be sea-meat!

Kah-Lan veers right and kicks hard.

His lungs ache. He's almost out of air. What will happen if he surfaces?

His body forces him up to breathe. He pops only his head above water.

Taking a breath, he blinks. The dark shape is a long, flat piece of wood. A furless pup is standing on its hind legs in the middle. The pup is holding a long branch with a flipper end and paddling away. It's heading toward another piece of wood with a furless Elder on it.

Safe.

Kah-Lan's pounding heart slows down. He swims to a protected cove and floats on his back. With his paws and flippers out of the water to keep them warm, he rests.

Soon his stomach demands sea-meat. Kah-Lan dives to the sea floor. Right away he finds mussels. He grips one with his paws and tugs.

And twists.

And wrenches.

It's firmly attached to the rock and doesn't budge. Even using his teeth doesn't work.

Kah-Lan hunts for something else to eat. The only sea-meat here is mussels. He grabs another one of the shelled creatures and pulls with all his strength. He cannot get it loose.

But Kah-Lan must eat a lot to stay warm in the cold ocean.

At the surface, Kah-Lan thinks of using a rock to pry the mussels free. He dives to fetch one. Kah-Lan whacks a mussel with the rock until it finally breaks away. Then another, and one more, tucking them in his left pouch. Holding the rock, he kicks his flippers and aims for the sky.

After smashing each mussel on his chest rock, Kah-Lan gobbles the fleshy insides. This sea-meat is extra tasty. He quickly dives down to chip more mussels off the rocks.

Kah-Lan surfaces and can't wait to eat them.

SPLASH.

Kah-Lan's heart races.

He twists around and drops his sea-meat and rock.

It's a shark jumping, looking for food.

Chapter Five

Sharks don't eat sea otters, but Kah-Lan's mother taught him to avoid them. One bite can kill an otter.

What if the shark thinks he's a young sea lion?

Kah-Lan needs a sea-tree forest to hide in. Or shore he can haul out on.

He can't smell any sea-trees. So he dashes toward land.

Is the shark chasing him underwater? Kah-Lan dares not check. He just keeps going.

Only the length of a drift-tree to go to shore now.

As soon as Kah-Lan's paws touch sand, he extends his claws and digs in. He scrambles onto the beach. Tripping over his flippers, he sprawls. Nose covered in sand, he clambers over rocks to get higher onto shore.

Kah-Lan's in no rush to return to the ocean. He'll wait until the shark gets its meal and is gone.

Finally he decides it's safe to go back. He stays in shallow water where sharks and orcas can't reach him.

Kah-Lan feels sleepy, but his coat is dirty. He needs to groom his fur many times during dawn and dark. Otherwise his skin will get wet and he'll get too cold. He could die. He starts combing bits of sea-meat out of his chest fur with his claws. A somersault rinses his coat. Once his chest is clean, Kah-Lan blows air into his underfur.

It takes him quite a while to groom every section of fur. Front and back, head to tail, all of his coat must be clean. Once he's done, he sleeps.

When Kah-Lan wakes, the sun has slipped away. Through dark, he hunts by touch, eats, grooms and sleeps again.

Before dawn, Kah-Lan feels rested. He can't wait to find other young male sea otters to raft with. In the dim light he swishes his back end and glides underwater along the coast.

On the other side of a rocky point, Kah-Lan surfaces. Grey clouds roll across the sky. His nostrils catch a whiff of sea otter. With a burst of energy he speeds forward, following the scent. A breeze ripples the water.

Kah-Lan stops and raises his head high to look over the small waves. The first rays of sunlight glint off two sleek brown heads. *Ow-u-ugh.*

Will they welcome him?

Both heads swivel. The young males stare at Kah-Lan.

They grunt in return. *U-um-ph, u-um-ph.* He rushes toward them.

Kah-Lan nudges the larger otter. He play-bites Kah-Lan's neck. Kah-Lan twists away from his sharp white teeth. The other otter—a bit smaller than Kah-Lan—nips his tail, so Kah-Lan darts off. Both chase Kah-Lan. They all wrestle, splashing and grunting.

Full of joy over his new raft, Kah-Lan
bunts the males toward the hunting
waters he discovered. Zid, the larger
otter, nips Kah-Lan's shoulder. It's no
play bite. Kah-Lan squeals.

Zid growls, making it clear he's in charge.
He will decide where they travel, eat and
rest. Kah-Lan paddles backward. Zid is
bigger than he is, so likely older. Kah-Lan
is relieved to have other sea otters to
raft with. He's happy to have a leader.

Zid leads Kah-Lan and Gula in the opposite direction. The sea is growing choppy. Soon they reach a clam bed brimming with sea-meat. Over and over the otters dive. Their whiskers sense their prey and their paws quickly dig out the clams. Back at the surface they whack, splash, crack and slurp.

The end of Gula's left big biting tooth is missing. It makes him look like a Grand otter. How did he break the tip? Did he chomp a too-hard shell?

The wind gains strength. It whips the sea into massive waves. Fat raindrops splatter the otters. It's time to groom, but first they must find a sheltered area.

Zid whistles, then paddles off at the surface. Gula and Kah-Lan follow him. A wave washes over Zid. He shakes his head, spraying water all around.

Kah-Lan can hardly see Zid through the heavy rain. But then Zid leaps and bolts underwater. Kah-Lan and Gula dive and pump their flippers to chase his bubble trail.

Kah-Lan swims at top speed to keep the stronger sea otter in sight.

Kah-Lan bobs for a breath. *Slam.* A sharp chunk of drift-tree hits his right shoulder. It hurts, but he must keep swimming. The next time he surfaces for air, a white object floats past his nose. He speed-weaves around the strands of fish-web hanging down from the object.

Where is Zid? Underwater, Kah-Lan bulges his eyes to see better. Finally he spots Zid's bubble trail and darts after him. When he peeks back, he's relieved to see that Gula is following too.

Kah-Lan's flippers ache, but he keeps pushing against the water. The next time his head is above the surface, he sees where they are and can't believe what Zid is doing. He's leading them straight into the swells, farther away from shore. Fear squeezes Kah-Lan's chest. Where is Zid taking them?

Chapter Six

Kah-Lan slips underwater, paddling hard. He doesn't know if he should follow Zid or head back toward shore on his own.

Kah-Lan keeps following. The sea otters swim on and on. Gula slips farther behind.

Later, when Kah-Lan surfaces to breathe, he crests a giant swell. He catches sight of an island. It has land-trees. A tall white object has a red top way up high above the trees. Over and over it flashes a light as bright as the sun. The island should give them shelter. Zid *does* know what he's doing.

The island blocks most of the wind. So the closer they swim to land, the smaller the swells. Near the island's rocky shoreline, the ocean still churns. Even with all of the white foam on the water, it's safer here than where the otters had been.

Ow-u-ugh. Kah-Lan grunts with delight when Gula appears.

Despite being exhausted, the otters all hunt, eat and groom. Kah-Lan finds a small rock big enough to pound mussels on.

The storm rages. Kah-Lan feels safe on this side of the island. When Zid links paws with him and Gula, Kah-Lan is content. Now he won't lose his raft.

Sometime during dark, the storm peaks.

In the growing light, Kah-Lan's belly cries for more food. He dives to hunt. After surfacing with a few mussels, he pulls out the chest rock he'd kept in his pouch all during dark. Zid and Gula start feeding too.

When Kah-Lan pops up from his next dive clutching a purple sea urchin, he's so surprised he almost drops it. On the edge of the island are a furless Elder and pup. How did they get all the way out here?

The furless pup points at Kah-Lan and squeals: *Take a picture, Daddy.*

Jumping up and down, the pup sounds excited. The fur atop its head whips in the wind. The furless Elder holds up a slim black object that clicks.

Kah-Lan avoids the urchin's spines while squeezing its shell. After it splits, he scrapes out the flesh and devours the sea-meat.

When Zid and Gula surface, the furless pup squeals again.

Click. Click.

Zid growls. Knowing the clicks do no harm, Kah-Lan coos. But Zid growls again.

The slim black object sings like a bird. The Elder holds it up to its ear, making deep sounds: *Hi, Jill...A Mayday call? Coming.*

The Elder grabs the paw of the furless pup. They run toward the tall red-and-white object.

Zid bunts Kah-Lan and Gula away from the island. With Zid in the lead, they paddle back toward the coast. Swimming with the wind, the otters can ride the swells.

Kah-Lan's muscles don't ache as they did swimming into the storm.

Eventually, land-trees come into view. The otters surf the waves as they get closer to shore. Will Zid guide them back to the clam bed? No, he turns in the other direction and dips underwater. Kah-Lan and Gula follow.

Farther along the coast they travel. The sun continues its journey through the sky.

The sound of water and air shooting up high makes Kah-Lan's heart pound. He looks back.

It's an orca spouting, heading their way!

Zid screeches a warning. They must hide in sea-trees or haul out on shore. Now.

But there is no sea-tree forest here. And these rocks are too steep to climb.

The otters streak along the rocky coast to escape their enemy.

Whoosh. The orca speeds after them. The otters swiftly paddle closer to shore.

At the surface, Zid whistles, urging Kah-Lan and Gula to go faster. Kah-Lan desperately pumps his flippers. His legs quiver.

Rounding a rocky point, Zid almost crashes into something smooth and reddish brown. He veers just in time and then swims alongside it.

When Kah-Lan grabs a breath, he glances upward. His pace slows. The reddish brown turns to black higher up. It's a stiff shiny creature the size of a cliff. He's never seen a creature so huge.

The orca is still pursuing them. Kah-Lan flees, his flippers straining to move at top speed again.

Zid swims the length of the shiny creature, then leads the otters around its end. But something looks wrong with the water.

What is that up ahead?

The sea otters are aiming directly at grey stink-ink.

Yet the orca is gaining on them and there's nowhere else to go.

At the surface, Kah-Lan flinches at the stench. It's worse than what he smelled in the bay with the struggling seagull. Ahead, a rainbow-tinted sheen covers the ocean.

The orca chases the otters closer to the stink-ink.

In a flash, Kah-Lan remembers that the stink-ink stopped the bird from flying. Did the furless ones make the booming noises to warn him of danger?

Zid bobs up in the stink-ink. He lets out a sickening squeal.

Is the stink-ink only floating on the surface? Kah-Lan dives, trying to swim below the stink-ink. Will Gula follow?

Chapter Seven

Gula does not follow Kah-Lan underwater. From below, Kah-Lan can see the shapes of Gula and Zid at the surface.

When the orca reaches the stink-ink, it twists and thrashes. Then it swims out to sea.

Above him, Kah-Lan sees stink-ink in every direction. Is it a bigger danger than the orca?

Kah-Lan paddles as hard as he can to get out from under the stink-ink. But he's running low on air. He aims for a bright spot where the water seems to be clear.

Almost there. Kah-Lan's lungs scream. He fights to keep swimming underwater, but he must breathe. Now.

Kah-Lan pops his nose above the surface for a small breath. He gags, then dives. Kicking his flippers, he finally reaches the clean sea water and surfaces.

Safe.

No, not safe yet. Breathing here is a little better, but his head and upper back are coated with stink-ink.

Furless Elders appear way up on the top edge of the shiny creature. One points at Zid and Gula floating in the stink-ink. The Elder makes loud noises:

*Oiled otters! We have to call Marine
Mammal Rescue.*

Kah-Lan is confused by the noises.
The stink-ink is spreading. It seems to
be coming out of the shiny creature.
Frightened, he whistles to Zid and Gula.
They must get away.

Zid and Gula turn toward Kah-Lan and dive. Soon they join him in the clean water. Stink-ink covers most of their fur.

Gula gags and coughs. He slowly rolls at the surface. Kah-Lan and Zid dive and somersault, but none of the stink-ink washes away.

They all claw and lick their fur, trying to clean off the stink-ink. Kah-Lan can only remove a little from his fur. The stink-ink is slick on his tongue and hurts his throat. He tries coughing up the horrible gunk but swallows a lot.

His stomach starts churning. His fur clumps. He's losing the air bubbles he'd carefully blown and whisked into his fur. Cold sea water burrows through his underfur. It trickles onto the skin on his back and head that has never been wet. Kah-Lan shivers from the chill.

Zid and Gula cough and gag as they also struggle to clean their coats.

With so little air trapped in their underfur, the sea otters start to sink. It takes great effort to stay at the surface.

Kah-Lan sneezes. His flippers and paws grow colder as he can no longer keep them out of the water while floating on his back. The stench makes it hard to breathe. Shivers turn to shuddering.

An orca-length shiny creature with two furless Elders on its back roars toward the sea otters. It will reach Gula first. His eyes are closed.

Zid and Kah-Lan squeal warnings to Gula. Zid begins swimming toward the sandy beach. Rubbing fur in the sand might remove the stink-ink. Kah-Lan paddles after Zid, with Gula weakly following them.

Kah-Lan turns back, cooing to encourage Gula onward. The furless ones have almost reached Gula.

He stops moving and sinks.

A furless Elder holds out a long branch with a web on the end, dipping it below Gula. Kah-Lan chomps his teeth at the furless Elder, but it doesn't back away. Instead it scoops up Gula with the web and lifts him onto the shiny creature. The Elder looks at Kah-Lan and calls softly: *Now you, buddy. We just want to get you clean.*

Kah-Lan growls and backs off.

Zid whistles. Kah-Lan turns and paddles toward the beach. But the shiny creature stiffly swims after him. He must go faster or he'll be caught too. Kah-Lan kicks as hard as he can.

Zid squeal-croaks in time to warn Kah-Lan of the web reaching for him.

He dives. But when he surfaces, the web attacks him again. Kah-Lan snarls. He thrusts his flippers, rising partway out of the water with his jaw open. He aims for the furless Elder's paw, but instead he bites the web. His powerful teeth rip it apart.

Kah-Lan feebly paddles beneath the waves toward shore. He's exhausted. His stomach churns and his throat stings. Kah-Lan's paws touch the sand. With his last energy he hauls himself up onto the beach.

Kah-Lan rolls over. All he can manage is to gently rub his upper back in the sand. It's not enough pressure to remove the stink-ink from his fur. Shivering, he collapses next to Zid. Kah-Lan closes his eyes, unable to move.

Chapter Eight

Kah-Lan stretches in the sand. He blinks in the light of dawn. Instead of shivering, he's warmer than he's ever felt before. He pants and shoves his flippers into the wet sand to cool down.

He pricks his ears. Something crunches in the sand behind him, getting closer. Kah-Lan whimpers. Zid lies still beside him.

Kah-Lan feels pressure around his chest. He growls. It sounds like a croak.

Something lifts him off the sand. He turns and stares into the face of a furless Elder. His squeal comes out as a whine.

More furless Elders appear. One has silver fur on its head. Silver-fur and the others have smooth purple paws.

Silver-fur calls: *How much of that otter is oiled?*

The furless one holding Kah-Lan looks away, making high-pitched sounds: *Just the upper back and head. But the one on the ground is covered.*

There's a brown tail at the back of this furless one's head. Kah-Lan tries to bite Head-tail's paw but is too weak to reach. He growl-croaks.

Head-tail makes gentle noises: *Relax, little guy. We're here to help.*

Kah-Lan's heart knocks hard against his chest. He can barely hear himself grumble.

He wriggles, but he can't escape Head-tail's grasp. What will this furless one do?

Head-tail shoves Kah-Lan into a cave. He twists his neck and sees Head-tail block the opening with a web. He tries to stand but doesn't have the energy. Instead he stretches his leg until he can touch the web with his flipper. The web is hard. Kah-Lan is trapped! He whimpers. All he wants to do is sleep. But furless ones pick up his web-cave and slide it into a dimly lit space.

Kah-Lan panics. Then a familiar smell hits his nostrils. Clam, already out of its shell. Head-tail swings the web open and extends its purple paw toward him. It's holding a piece of the sea-meat. But Kah-Lan's stomach still churns from the stink-ink. He turns his nose away.

Head-tail removes the food, pours small rocks around Kah-Lan, then closes the web. No, the rocks aren't rocks. They're hard. Cold. Clear. Kah-Lan bites one. It cracks apart and turns wet. It tastes like rain. He shuts his eyes. The rain-rocks feel soothing as they cool his body.

Kah-Lan startles when furless Elders slide another web-cave next to his. He sniffs Zid's scent mixed with stink-ink stench. Kah-Lan coos. Zid does not respond. Is he alive?

One more web-cave is on the ground. Gula is inside. Kah-Lan coos as loudly as he can, then whistles weakly. But there's no answer from Gula. Silver-fur bends down and attaches a thin, clear strand to Gula. Furless ones pick up his web-cave and gently set it beside Zid's.

Does Gula feel worse than Kah-Lan?

Kah-Lan sees furless Elders bring sea-meat to Zid and Gula. Neither otter stirs. The furless ones take the food away. Head-tail adds rain-rocks to each web-cave.

Silver-fur calls out: *Strap down the kennels. We don't want them sliding around.*

The bumpy ride will be hard enough on the otters.

The others grab long yellow strands like sea-tree blades. They wrap them around the web-caves. One strand stretches across the web on Kah-Lan's web-cave.

Kah-Lan wonders how he can get back into the ocean.

BANG. BANG. He flinches as the furless ones make the space darker. He can no longer see the sky.

A rumbling noise like a shiny creature's roar makes Kah-Lan squeal-croak. He can faintly hear the voices of the furless Elders. Then his web-cave starts moving. Everything under and around him jiggles. His heart races.

His web-cave bumps into Zid's. When Kah-Lan whines, Zid whimpers. Alive.

Gula is silent.

Eventually the rattling stops. But Kah-Lan feels as if his web-cave is still moving. He's so warm he shifts around to sprawl on top of the cold rain-rocks. Then sleep takes him.

⟋⟍

Kah-Lan stirs. The rain-rocks are gone and his paws and flippers are wet. He feels too warm again. His stomach still churns. His web-cave stops moving.

A furless one calls: *I'll buy more ice. Can you try feeding them again?*

Kah-Lan blinks as sunlight streams in. He sniffs the air. No ocean smell. He trembles. Where is he? The strongest scents are land-trees and the stink-ink on his fur.

Head-tail opens the web on Kah-Lan's web-cave. Its purple paw holds out a piece of clam. Kah-Lan backs away. Head-tail drops it in front of him. He is starved, so he snatches it. He barely chews before gulping it down.

Head-tail drops more clams and he devours them. He has a little more energy after eating.

Rain-rocks and sea-meat. Both things from the furless ones make Kah-Lan feel better.

Then Head-tail offers Kah-Lan curved orange things he's never seen before. He refuses the orange-curves.

Silver-fur pulls the web open on Zid's web-cave. Kah-Lan smells clam. But Zid growl-croaks.

Kah-Lan coos to encourage Zid to eat. Zid growls again. Kah-Lan coos once more. Zid kicks the side of his web-cave, nudging Kah-Lan's.

Silver-fur takes the food away, making low, gentle sounds: *The far one's still not stirring. The IV fluids should help. I hope he makes it to Vancouver.*

Head-tail brings more rain-rocks. Kah-Lan shoves his head under them. They are cold and refreshing.

More motion. Whining.

Sleeping. Warmth.

Rain-rocks. Coolness.

The next time Head-tail offers clams on its paw, Kah-Lan hesitates. But then he snatches them and backs off to eat. He slurps and chews loudly so Zid can hear him. Finally Zid accepts the clams, but not without a low growl. He gives Kah-Lan a weak coo.

Then Kah-Lan hears a faint cough. Is that Gula? Kah-Lan and Zid both coo. Kah-Lan hears a raspy sound from the far web-cave. Is that Gula breathing? He coos to Gula again.

When Head-tail offers Kah-Lan some orange-curves, he's too hungry to refuse. He grabs them and almost swallows them whole. The taste reminds him of crab. He gobbles more from Head-tail's purple paw.

Head-tail makes a cooing sound: *You like the shrimp, do you?*

Soon Kah-Lan's web-cave is moving again. He should groom. But he's so tired. He sneezes and something thick oozes out of his nose. Kah-Lan wipes the stickiness away with his paw. He tries grooming. But his tongue hits stink-ink. He gags and gives up.

The movement stops again. A seagull screeches. Are they back at the ocean?

A loud roar startles Kah-Lan. He hears deep rumbling. His web-cave moves again. But it feels like it's floating on water, swaying side to side. What's happening?

After a long time the rumbling finally slows. A thundering blast makes Kah-Lan squeal-croak. The movement stops. *Clank. Rumble. Creak.*

What's happening? Will they survive?

Chapter Nine

The sounds and motion return to what Kah-Lan experienced when they first left the beach. Yet he can no longer smell the ocean. He's breathing much faster than usual. He's so weary he can't keep his eyes open.

Later, after his web-cave stops moving, light floods in. Kah-Lan squints. He feels much too warm. Furless Elders pick up his web-cave and carry it some distance.

Through the web Kah-Lan can see the sun high in the sky.

His eyelids are heavy. He has no energy to growl. He smells the sea and coughs. Is that a seal snorting? His nose leaks again.

The furless Elders set his web-cave down. Kah-Lan tries to stand but isn't strong enough. They swing back the web and tip the web-cave forward. Kah-Lan slides out the opening onto smooth wood. Next to his head is a round black shell filled with rain water. All around this new space is silver web, even above him. He can see the clouds through the holes in the web.

Head-tail offers Kah-Lan some mussels already out of their shells. Although his stomach is still churning, he eats. The furless ones keep helping. But what else will they do?

A shorter furless Elder arrives. It has a black tail out the back of its head. Black-tail stares at Kah-Lan, making soft high-pitched noises: *What can I do?*

Head-tail quietly replies: *Cover them with ice cubes. They're hyperthermic. We need to lower their body temperature. They're likely sick with pneumonia too. We'll test for that tomorrow.*

With more rain-rocks surrounding Kah-Lan, he sleeps until dark. He hears Zid and Gula coughing nearby.

～❧

Come dawn, even with so much sleep, Kah-Lan is exhausted. Head-tail sits nearby watching him. Kah-Lan raises his head. He can see Zid and Gula each in their own space like his. He coos to them, but they don't respond.

Silver-fur appears and opens part of the web around Kah-Lan's space, then walks in. Head-tail covers Kah-Lan's head with something soft. He chomps at the furless ones and squirms. What are they doing? He feels a sharp pinch in his hind leg and snarl-croaks. The furless ones uncover his head and leave him alone.

Kah-Lan looks up, frightened. It feels like the web above him is spinning. He quickly gets so drowsy he falls asleep.

Later, when Kah-Lan opens his eyes, the sun is way up in the sky. He's too weak to stand.

Head-tail and other furless ones roll him onto his back. They hold him down—his head, upper body, lower body. He grumbles and wriggles, fighting against them, but they only press harder. Head-tail slips a long, clear object like a sea-tree stem into his mouth and keeps sliding it down his throat. He tries to bite it, to shift his head, to kick his flippers.

Then Head-tail pours something black down the clear stem and pulls the stem out. The furless ones roll Kah-Lan over and leave him alone. Did they put clear stems inside Zid and Gula too?

After a while the churning in Kah-Lan's stomach lessens. When Head-tail offers him orange-curve mush, he devours it all, even though it has a slightly odd taste. Squid and more clams come next. Kah-Lan starts feeling stronger.

A seagull perches on the silver web above him, screeching. But the gaps are too small for the bird to get through to steal the sea-meat. After Kah-Lan finishes eating, Head-tail carries orange-curve mush to Zid's space.

Zid growls. Kah-Lan coos to urge him to eat.

Head-tail calls softly: *No clams until you eat your medicine.*

Zid snarls. Head-tail moans and leaves with the mush.

Kah-Lan's eyelids droop and he drifts off.

The sun is low in the sky when Kah-Lan wakes next. After another meal he whistles to Zid and Gula. If they won't eat, they can't get stronger.

Kah-Lan hears slurping and grunts. Is that Zid eating orange-curve mush?

Kah-Lan feels cooler and less tired. He shuffles around his space for the first time.

Ow-u-ugh. Water! He dives in. It's like rain, not salty. Cold—just how he likes it.

He swims to the bottom. It is firm and level, and not far down. There are no rocks. There is no sand or sea-meat.

At the surface, one kick of his flippers takes him most of the way across the pool of water. Such a small space. Kah-Lan yearns for the ocean where he can paddle freely. But even this short swim wears him out. With stink-ink on his head and back, his skin is now wet and cold. He climbs out onto the wood to warm up and shuts his eyes.

The sound of a splash close by wakes Kah-Lan. Zid has a pool too. Kah-Lan lurches to the edge of his space closest to Zid's. He bites at the silver web, trying to get to Zid. When he coos, Zid grunts. But Kah-Lan hears only coughing from Gula.

Black-tail looks on as Kah-Lan grooms his chest and legs. Even the thought of licking the fur on his head makes him gag. So he ignores the soiled parts of his coat.

~ close by ~

Kah-Lan sleeps and wakes often during dark. Gula is silent. Kah-Lan whines and coos to him.

Head-tail brings more sea-meat the next dawn. Kah-Lan hears strange thumping from Gula's direction. Why is he making that noise? What's wrong? Kah-Lan's heart thuds wildly as he coos to Gula.

Head-tail runs toward Gula, calling: *The youngest one is convulsing. Not sure we can save him.*

The thumping stops. No more raspy breathing or coughing from Gula.

Later, furless Elders carry Gula away on a flat piece of wood. When they pass by, Kah-Lan sniffs. Gula has an unusual scent. He is lying down with his mouth hanging open, tipless tooth showing. He's not moving. Kah-Lan and Zid coo to him. But Gula does not respond. Kah-Lan whimpers. He remembers a similar scent coming from a Grand otter who had died.

Did the furless ones kill Gula? Or did he die from the stink-ink?

Kah-Lan only found Gula a few dawns ago. Now he's gone. Will Zid die here too? Will Kah-Lan?

It takes a long time for Kah-Lan to feel like eating again. Before he's offered clams or other sea-meat, he's always given the orange-curve mush with the strange taste. And always there is a furless one close by watching, even through dark. Often it pulls out a slim black object that clicks, just like other furless ones Kah-Lan has encountered. During dark the object also flashes a bright light.

By dawn, Kah-Lan can bound over to his pool and leap in. He can paddle faster at the surface. Black-tail watches from outside Kah-Lan's space. Head-tail approaches.

Black-tail stands up, making a quiet sound: *What's the plan?*

Head-tail opens part of the web and walks into Kah-Lan's space, responding: *He's stable enough for us to clean his fur.*

There's a branch in Head-tail's purple paws. The branch has a web on the end. It's what the furless ones used to snatch Gula out of the ocean. Kah-Lan chomps at the branch.

They move closer to Kah-Lan. He dives and kicks his flippers. But Head-tail rushes around and slips the web under him. He thrashes about. Kah-Lan is caught!

Head-tail scoops him out of the pool and sets him on the smooth wood. Furless Elders hide behind flat pieces of wood and herd Kah-Lan against the silver web.

Now Silver-fur arrives. Black-tail covers Kah-Lan's head and presses down. After a sharp poke in his hind leg, Kah-Lan snarls. The furless ones rapidly back out of his space.

Kah-Lan's head feels light and everything looks blurry. Did this happen to Gula? Is this how it feels to die?

His eyelids droop. Kah-Lan feels like he's floating and whistles to Zid.

Chapter Ten

When Kah-Lan wakes up, he's in a different spot on the wood in his space. His fur is dry and smells sweeter than rain. Reaching behind, he pulls his back fur to his mouth. There's not a bit of stink-ink. Did the furless Elders clean Kah-Lan? The stink-ink is gone from the wood too. Kah-Lan rolls and stretches. *Ow-u-ugh.*

Silver-fur and the other furless Elders walk toward Zid's space. Kah-Lan scrambles over as close as he can get to Zid. He presses his nose against the silver web.

Splash. Zid dives into his pool. He surfaces, growling fiercely. The furless Elders scoop Zid with a web on a branch. He twists about but they haul him out of the water. Zid bares his teeth and bites. He narrowly misses a furless one's paw, biting the web instead.

Whatever the furless ones do to Kah-Lan, they do to Zid. Will the furless ones clean Zid's fur now? Kah-Lan coos to Zid to calm him as the furless ones gather around him.

The furless Elders leave. Zid grumbles. He staggers around and collapses. Is Zid hurt?

Then Zid is silent.

After a short while the furless ones return and carry Zid away.

Kah-Lan squeals and never leaves the silver web. Seals snort nearby. A breeze brings the scent of the ocean, making him long for home. Here there are smells like stink-ink too, but not as powerful. Deep clanking sounds come from far away.

What's happening to Zid?

Finally he reappears, still asleep. Kah-Lan stands on his flippers with his paws on the silver web so he can see Zid better. His fur looks dry. The furless Elders set him down in his space. They must have cleaned him too.

Zid wakes up making a low growl. But when he sniffs his fur, he grunts with delight.

Soon Head-tail returns and feeds Kah-Lan orange-curve mush. Then Head-tail tosses sea-meat into his pool. Kah-Lan dives in. The water is a little salty.

He easily retrieves the food. Will Kah-Lan and Zid ever get back to the ocean and hunt for sea-meat again?

The next time Head-tail walks toward Kah-Lan's space, he leaps into the pool. He's ready to eat.

～∂

Through many dawns and darks, Kah-Lan and Zid remain in their separate areas.

Gradually Zid stops growling at the furless Elders. He no longer chomps at them. Both sea otters grow stronger. They eat, groom, sleep and repeat.

Silver-fur appears. Kah-Lan feels a sharp pinch on his hind leg again and is confused. He just groomed all his fur. Why do the furless ones need to clean it again? His eyelids close.

When Kah-Lan wakes up later, he has no idea what the furless ones did to him. But he does smell a delicious scent he hasn't sniffed since leaving the ocean—crab. He devours every last morsel and yearns for good hunting waters.

Black-tail makes excited sounds: *The vet says you and your buddy can share an enclosure.*

Kah-Lan makes a low growl when furless Elders arrive with a web-cave. They herd Kah-Lan inside and close the web. He screeches, twisting from one end of the web-cave to the other. His heart races as he recalls moving and jiggling for a long time in that dim space.

But the furless ones do not carry him far. They tip him out onto flat wood next to a large pool. *Splash.* Kah-Lan dives into the sea water.

Soon another web-cave arrives—with
Zid inside. When the furless one opens
the web on his web-cave, Zid leaps
straight into the water. Kah-Lan and
Zid wrestle and coo. They float on their
backs beside each other and link paws.

Several dawns later, furless Elders arrive but have no sea-meat. Zid whistles and dives to the bottom of their pool.

Kah-Lan spots Silver-fur. As much as he dislikes the poke in the leg, he did get to eat crab when he woke up the last time.

But after the leg pinch and sleep, Kah-Lan finds no crab. And no Zid. Instead there's a hard orange tag stuck to his left flipper. He tries to shake it free. His flipper stings. Then he lifts the tag to his mouth, bites it and pulls, but it won't crack or budge. How did it get there? Will it ever come off?

The tag doesn't keep him from paddling. But he'd rather get rid of it.

A seagull screeches. The scent of the ocean wafts by, tickling Kah-Lan's nose. Hearing seals snort out there makes Kah-Lan long for freedom.

Zid returns. He has an orange tag on his left flipper too. When he wakes up he thrashes about, whipping the tag against the wood. Then he dives into the pool, twisting, chomping and swishing. But the tag stays whole and firmly attached.

Head-tail tosses a large amount of sea-meat into the pool. Kah-Lan and Zid gobble everything. After all of the diving, Kah-Lan hardly notices the tag. The sea otters carefully groom their coats.

Many furless Elders appear along with the familiar web-caves. Now what?

They herd the sea otters inside the web-caves and carry them back into a dim space like at the beach. Kah-Lan and Zid squeal in panic. Head-tail adds rain-rocks and makes soothing sounds: *Relax. It's only short drives and a flight. You'll like where you're going.*

But Kah-Lan remembers how horrible he felt in this space before. He was weak and exhausted. The stink-ink churned in his stomach. The jostling made him feel worse.

When the roar starts, Kah-Lan flinches. His web-cave begins moving. Both otters whine. Kah-Lan trembles.

Soon the movement stops. Kah-Lan can still smell the ocean. It's the same scent he's smelled for many dawns. Furless Elders pick up his web-cave and carry it toward the water.

Up ahead a big shiny creature is floating in the ocean. It has a huge body and outstretched wings like a giant seagull. The furless ones set Kah-Lan's web-cave inside the shiny-bird. They shove it into the dim space next to Zid's web-cave. Head-tail pours more rain-rocks on both sea otters. Zid and Kah-Lan growl.

Roar. Kah-Lan startles. The shiny-bird starts moving. The noise grows even louder. *Bump. Bump. Bump.* Then the shuddering stops and Kah-Lan feels his web-cave tilt. He slides against the web. The otters snarl.

Kah-Lan's web-cave stops tilting. The roar carries on and on. Zid screams. Kah-Lan squeals. This is the worst danger yet!

Finally, Kah-Lan senses his web-cave tilting the other way. The roar becomes quieter. What is happening?

Chapter Eleven

Whoosh. Kah-Lan hears water spraying, like a wave hitting a large rock. His web-cave is level again. The shudders return. He whimpers.

Once they stop moving, Kah-Lan can hear a furless one calling: *Load them into the truck.*

The space gets brighter. Kah-Lan can smell the ocean. It smells like *his* ocean. He bites at the web, trying to get free.

Furless Elders carry the web-caves out of the shiny-bird and set them onto a flat black area.

Roar. Rumble. They are moving again. Kah-Lan stares out the web at the sky and clouds. The tips of leaning land-trees come into view.

Soon the movement ends. Kah-Lan can hear waves crashing onshore. *Ow-u-ugh.* He pushes hard on the web with his paws. It doesn't budge. He claws the edge.

The furless Elders carry both web-caves down to the beach. Head-tail opens the web at the front of Kah-Lan's web-cave and makes a soft noise: *Good luck out there.*

The ocean is straight ahead.

Home!

As fast as their paws and flippers can take them, Kah-Lan and Zid scramble out.

Grunting, they stumble over rocks and grasses, aiming for the sea. Then they fling themselves into the surf and glide in the clear salt water.

No stink-ink!

An orca-sized shiny creature with furless ones on its back is floating off to the right. Kah-Lan and Zid head to the left.

Zid play-bites Kah-Lan's neck. Twisting away, Kah-Lan nips Zid on the tail. They wrestle and splash and grunt.

Then they hunt for sea-meat.

Sea urchins, and clams still in their shells!

Zid and Kah-Lan eat their fill, then groom their coats. They float on their backs, link paws and have a short rest.

But with no sea-trees here, it isn't safe to stay. It's time to find a new home.

Not knowing when they'll get food again, they dive for more before leaving.

Kah-Lan surfaces with a purple sea urchin and splits it open. After eating half of the mushy flesh, he glances around. No Zid. Kah-Lan scrapes out more with his paw.

Zid still doesn't appear. He's been underwater a long time.

Too long.

Kah-Lan drops his sea-meat and dives. The water is murky at the bottom. He bulges his eyes to see more clearly.

Where is Zid?

Turning, Kah-Lan spots a cloud of bubbles. Zid! He's head down, flippers a blur. Kah-Lan speeds over.

Zid's head is stuck through something thin and silver. It has a strand attached that's holding him down. He's trapped!

Kah-Lan bites the strand and twists. It shreds a little. He bites it again and pulls back. Then the strand snaps. Finally Zid's free.

Zid tries to swim to the sky, but he falters.

Is he running out of air?

Kah-Lan slips underneath Zid, pushing him upward. Kah-Lan pumps his flippers.

Kah-Lan's lungs cry for air.

Zid goes limp.

No, don't drown.

Gasp. Kah-Lan gulps air. Zid's head is above the surface, but his eyes are closed. He's not breathing.

Kah-Lan squeals and nips Zid on the shoulder. He doesn't move. So Kah-Lan bunts Zid hard in the stomach. It jars Zid enough that he sucks in air.

Alive.

Zid floats on his back. His breathing sounds raspy. The thin silver thing around Zid's neck is pressing on his throat. He gags. He can take only shallow breaths.

Zid needs help!

Kah-Lan tries to slide his teeth around the silver thing. It's too tight. Even if Kah-Lan could bite it, the silver thing seems too hard to break.

Kah-Lan remembers how furless Elders freed Snort. And warned Kah-Lan away from the stink-ink. And fed him and Zid, cleaned off the stink-ink and brought them home.

The only ones that can help Zid now are furless ones.

Kah-Lan coos to Zid.

If Kah-Lan leaves him, an orca could snatch Zid. But if Kah-Lan doesn't get help, Zid won't survive.

Kah-Lan dashes off toward the beach where Head-tail set them free. Once he's closer, he scans the area. There's no sign of furless ones.

But the shiny creature is still floating in the distance. He shallow-dives and streaks toward it just below the surface.

Reaching the stiff, shiny creature, Kah-Lan sees two furless Elders and a furless pup. They have branches with webs. The furless pup is standing on the nose of the shiny creature holding a skinny branch. A long thin strand hangs down from the end.

Kah-Lan squeals and whistles.

The pup calls: *Mom, there's a sea otter!*

One Elder clicks a slim black object.

Kah-Lan paddles backward toward Zid, squealing. Will they follow?

They stay put.

So Kah-Lan rushes back, whistling. The furless pup's strand is attached to a red-and-white object floating in the water. Kah-Lan grips the object with his paws and pulls it in Zid's direction.

The pup shrieks: *Hey, let go!*

A deep noise comes from the Elder with fur on its face: *What's going on?*

The furless pup calls: *The otter has my bobber. I think he wants us to follow him.*

Kah-Lan tugs harder. Then he drops the red-and-white object and squeals.

Fur-face calls: *We haven't caught any fish, so we might as well.*

The other Elder makes high-pitched noises: *But don't get too close.*

Rumble. Gurgle. The shiny creature starts swimming. The furless pup pulls in the red-and-white object and sits down.

Ow-u-ugh. Kah-Lan darts ahead, leading the furless ones toward Zid.

When Kah-Lan glances back, the shiny creature is still following. He bolts through the water.

Can Zid survive until they reach him?

Chapter Twelve

Zid's still floating.

Kah-Lan whistles, then hurries over to help Zid stay at the surface. As the furless ones approach, Zid growl-croaks but doesn't try to move away.

The shiny creature goes silent. Fur-face cries: *Look, that otter's got fishing gear around its neck. Get the wire cutters.*

The furless pup calls: *No, Dad, don't touch him. My teacher says they're dangerous.*

The other Elder responds: *I'm calling Marine Mammal Rescue.* It taps the black object with one paw.

Fur-face makes urgent sounds: *I'm not sure he'll survive until a rescuer gets here.*

The other Elder holds the black object up to its head and makes rapid noises: *Hello...Sea otter in distress...A bit south of there...Yes, another one...Both have orange flipper tags...Really?*

Zid coughs.

The shiny creature drifts toward him.

The Elder puts down the black object and cries: *A team released these otters today. They're still in the area and are on their way.*

Zid gags.

Kah-Lan screams in fright.

The furless pup coos: *Help will be here soon.* It keeps cooing.

Kah-Lan is confused. Why aren't they freeing Zid? He squeals.

The black object buzzes. The Elder calls into it: *He's still breathing...Yes, we'll pick you up.* It waves a paw toward land.

Rumble. Gurgle. The shiny creature starts backing away.

Kah-Lan grumbles.

Fur-face calls: *Hang on, you two. We'll be right back.*

The shiny creature races forward, heading to shore.

Zid's cough is more of a croak. Kah-Lan is frantic. Why did the furless ones leave?

The roar of the shiny creature becomes quieter.

Zid closes his eyes. He's taking only sips of air.

Kah-Lan whimpers.

How much longer can Zid live?

Kah-Lan links paws with him and coos.

A while later, a roar in the distance grows louder. Dropping Zid's paw, Kah-Lan raises his head higher out of the water. The shiny creature is returning.

It speeds directly to the otters. There are more furless ones on its back.

There's Head-tail!

Ow-u-ugh.

The shiny creature stops roaring and drifts toward the otters. Head-tail grabs a branch, dips the web under Zid and lifts him onto the shiny creature.

Kah-Lan squeals. From the water he can't see what the furless ones are doing to Zid.

Head-tail cries: *Cover his head with the blanket.*

Snip.

Head-tail holds up the hard silver thing, now broken apart. The furless pup shrieks. Head-tail lifts the branch with Zid still in the web, setting him in the ocean. He floats out of the web as Head-tail dips it downward and away from him.

Click. Click.

Zid swishes his tail and slowly paddles off, taking deeper breaths. He coughs. Kah-Lan joins him, cooing. He hooks his paw around one of Zid's.

Click. Click.

Head-tail gently calls: *Stay out of trouble, okay?*

When Zid's breathing calms, Kah-Lan dives. He brings up a sea urchin for Zid.

As Zid devours the sea-meat, Kah-Lan swims closer to the shiny creature. He leaps, diving straight down. Then he curves, paddling hard upward. He raises his head high out of the water. Looking at the furless ones, Kah-Lan grunts.

The furless pup jabs a curled paw up in the air and makes joyful sounds: *Yes! Your friend is okay.*

Rumble. Roar. The shiny creature swims away with the furless ones.

Once Zid recovers it's time for the sea otters to go too.

Zid tries to get Kah-Lan to paddle in the opposite direction from the shiny creature. Kah-Lan refuses. His instinct tells him to travel the same way as the furless ones, but go farther. Zid whistles. But then he submits and follows Kah-Lan.

When they see the shiny creature floating up ahead, Kah-Lan veers away. He leads Zid into deeper water. Kah-Lan is relieved to pass by the furless ones and leave them behind.

After swimming for a long while, Kah-Lan recognizes the place he found mussels. He dives and Zid follows. Below, Zid tries to pull the sea-meat away from the rock, but it won't budge. Grabbing a loose rock, Kah-Lan uses it to chip off mussels and fills his pouches. Zid does the same.

Later in their travels, Kah-Lan sees they are near the raft of mature male sea otters. He guides Zid well around them, checking for danger.

At Snort's reef Kah-Lan dives to check if Snort is there. No sign of the seal. But back at the surface, Kah-Lan hears a snort and spins around. He glides toward Snort.

Ow-u-ugh.

Another snort and Kah-Lan grunts once more. Snort must find plenty of fish here, but it's not suitable for Kah-Lan and Zid. They keep paddling along the coast.

Up ahead is Kah-Lan's old raft of females and pups. As he and Zid swim past, Kah-Lan spots his mother and Yamka. He coos to them. But—as he expects—they ignore him, treating him like any other young male.

Two other sea otters raise their heads higher above the water. Both race out to Kah-Lan and Zid. It's Myac and Wanu!

The young males tackle Kah-Lan, play-biting his face and shoulder. They stop wrestling and grunt to Zid. They do not return to the raft. Kah-Lan takes off, with Zid right behind.

At the surface, Kah-Lan flips onto his back. Myac and Wanu are not following him and Zid. Kah-Lan whistles and grunts. Will they join them?

Myac sprints after Kah-Lan.

Wanu raises his head higher above the surface. He whines. Then screeches. But finally he follows too.

Ow-u-ugh. Kah-Lan welcomes them to his raft.

Farther along the coast, Kah-Lan glimpses a white object before it dips behind a wave. He squeals a warning to the other otters. Cautiously, he paddles forward. Underwater, he finds a mass of fish-web strands attached to the white object. Kah-Lan bunts Wanu, Myac and Zid away from the danger.

The young male sea otters keep travelling together. They hunt, groom and rest when needed. But Kah-Lan keeps them moving.

Finally they discover a new home— a sea-tree forest far away from stink-ink and furless ones.

About Sea Otters

Sea otters (*Enhydra lutris*) are marine mammals that live in the North Pacific Ocean, along the coasts of Japan, Russia, Canada and the United States (Alaska, Washington and California).

These well-adapted animals spend their whole lives in the cold ocean near shore. Sea otters dive for food, eat, groom, play, float, mate, give birth and sleep in the water. They haul out on land, ice or rocks when injured, ill, in extreme danger or to conserve energy. They make their homes in kelp forests and bays, usually in rocky areas.

A group of sea otters—called a raft—may link paws to stay together, or wrap themselves with kelp to keep from drifting when they rest. Rafts of female sea otters and their pups stay together, while males form separate groups. A mother will usually have only one pup at a time, and she devotes six months to a year to caring for and teaching her pup. Weaned males leave their raft of females and pups and travel on their own, eventually joining a raft of males.

To keep warm in the ocean, sea otters must eat a huge amount of seafood. While sea otters reduce the abundance of shellfish in a location, they do not eat all of the shellfish, leaving enough of the creatures to repopulate the area. Sea otters dive to the ocean floor and search with their front paws and sensitive whiskers. Sea otters' hind feet are long webbed flippers to help them swim and dive. These animals are able to stay underwater four to five minutes before returning to the surface to breathe again, but most foraging dives last one minute or less.

Sea otters carry their catch in their pouch, a fold of loose skin under each foreleg. At the surface they float on their back to eat their prey, using their stomach as a table. When their powerful teeth aren't strong enough to break a hard shell, sea otters will hold a rock on their chest and bang the shell against it.

Sea otters must spend a lot of time cleaning their coat and blowing air into their thick underfur. Long guard hairs keep the underfur and skin dry, and the trapped air helps the animals stay warm. Sea otters grunt or coo when content or excited; whine when frustrated; and squeal, growl, whistle, grumble or chomp their teeth when frightened or distressed.

A few hundred years ago sea otters were plentiful. Then hunters discovered their fur, the thickest coat of all animals. By the early 1900s, sea otters were nearly extinct and governments stepped in to protect the few small, isolated groups that remained. In Alaska the sea otter population grew significantly over the following decades, and in the 1960s and 1970s some Alaskan sea otters were relocated to suitable coastal waters elsewhere in Alaska as well as to British Columbia, Washington and Oregon. Today there are approximately 110,000 sea otters in the world. In the United States, sea otters are listed as threatened, while in Canada they are listed as a species of special concern, which means sea otters could become threatened or endangered.

Besides danger from natural predators, sea otters can drown by getting tangled in fishing equipment or be harmed by pollution or by plastic garbage and parasites entering the ocean. But today the greatest threat to sea otters is an oil spill. Oil quickly soils a sea otter's coat, allowing cold water to reach the sea otter's skin. As the sea otter tries to clean its fur, it breathes and swallows the harmful oil. After a spill of crude oil, marine fuel, diesel or canola oil, a sea otter will not survive without help from trained marine mammal experts. However, in a spill of diluted bitumen, with its thick unrefined tar and volatile solvents creating toxic fumes, a sea otter will not survive long enough to be rescued.

In this story, Kah-Lan and Zid survived a small diesel spill because the Vancouver Aquarium's Marine Mammal Rescue Centre (MMRC) was notified by the oil tanker workers in time for MMRC staff to rescue the sea otters before they died from their exposure to the fuel.

Rehabilitation at MMRC takes a few weeks, or longer, depending on many variables, including the initial condition of the sea otter. If the animal ingested oil during exposure or by grooming its oiled coat, staff would give it activated charcoal through a feeding tube. Antibiotics to treat pneumonia are usually hidden in the sea otter's food, often mixed with shrimp-based products. A staff member or volunteer observes the sea otter twenty-four hours a day. The goal is to release the animal back where it was rescued as soon as possible. Before release, the sea otter is sedated to be tagged with an identification flipper tag.

It is illegal and dangerous to approach, touch or move sea otters. People should stay at least 100 metres away from sea otters. This is for the safety of the animals and the public. Sea otters have extremely sharp teeth and powerful jaws—designed to crack hard-shelled prey—and therefore their strong bite can crush a person's hand, easily breaking bones. As the number of sea otters increases and the animals spread farther along North America's west coast, interactions with humans will become more common. If you discover a sea otter in distress, contact the nearest marine mammal rescue agency.

Author's Note

In writing *Kah-Lan and the Stink-Ink*, I imagined how sea otters would respond in action and thought. What would they do in order to survive? I remained true to the natural behaviour of sea otters, except for taking artistic licence with the following:

- In reality, older male sea otters might not growl at a young male sea otter approaching their raft.

- While orcas do prey on sea otters in some locations in Alaska, orcas are not generally a real threat to sea otters in British Columbia. Both transient and resident orcas are found in the waters off the west coast of Vancouver Island, B.C., where the story is set. Resident orcas eat only fish while transient orcas eat marine mammals.

- Great white sharks are a serious threat to sea otters in California, but not to sea otters in British Columbia.

Acknowledgements

The Vancouver Aquarium introduced me to sea otters many years ago. The more I learned about these amazing, resilient marine mammals, the more deeply I grew to love, respect and want to write about and protect them.

Will Autio, the first person I want to show my writing to, shared insights about this story and provided unfailing support. Critiquers par excellence Eileen Holland,

Leeann Zouras, Lisa Dunlop, Loraine Kemp, Mary Ann Thompson, Michèle Griskey, Patricia Fraser and Stefan Autio read one or more drafts of the outline and/or story and gave me valuable feedback.

Lindsaye Akhurst (Head-tail) and Dr. Martin Haulena (Silver-fur) of the Vancouver Aquarium's Marine Mammal Rescue Centre, Vancouver, B.C., explained their important work when I toured the centre, and answered my many questions about sea otters, seals and the rescue and rehabilitation process. A shout-out of thanks to Lindsaye and Isabelle Groc for their enthusiasm for this story, reviewing it for accuracy and clarifying research details via email.

Lighthouse keepers Caroline Woodward and Jeff George shared the story and photos of a sea otter that took refuge in a storm near their home on Lennard Island, B.C., and reviewed the manuscript for accuracy of details about the west coast of Vancouver Island.

Melanie Jeffs of Crwth Press embraced the manuscript, and through her editorial vision and skills, made it better. Teresa Bubela guided the book's development with her talented artistic direction, and designed a beautiful book layout. Dawn Loewen masterfully applied her impeccable copy editing and Audrey McClellan provided careful proofreading. Emma Pedersen created the delightful cover and active interior illustrations that convey my characters so well.

My heartfelt thanks to everyone in my raft who helped me strengthen this story and get it into readers' hands.

KAREN AUTIO grew up horse-crazy and book-loving in Nipigon, Ontario. She fell in love with sea otters in 1984 on her first visit to the Vancouver Aquarium. When she's not researching, writing or working as a freelance editor, Karen enjoys canoeing, photographing wildlife, reading and travelling. She delights in revealing nuggets of little-known Canadian history and natural history in her classroom presentations. Karen lives in Kelowna, British Columbia. To learn more about Karen and her books, visit www.karenautio.com.

EMMA PEDERSEN is a graduate of the OCAD University drawing and painting program. Her playful style infuses character and story into each illustration. Emma lives with her husband in an apartment full of books in Toronto, Ontario. For more information, visit www.epillustration.com.

About Crwth Press

Crwth (pronounced crooth) Press is a small independent publisher based in British Columbia. A crwth is a Welsh stringed instrument that was commonly played in Wales until the mid-1800s, when it was replaced by the violin. We chose this word for the company name because we like the way music brings people together, and we want our press to do the same.

Crwth Press is committed to sustainability and accessibility. This book is printed in Canada on 100 percent post-consumer waste paper using only vegetable-based inks. For more on our sustainability model, visit www.crwth.ca.

To make our books accessible, we use fonts that individuals with dyslexia find easier to read. The font for this book is Lexie Readable.